A North-South Paperback

This book is dedicated to "The Three Bears" –
Bert, Bernadette and Bernard

GOLDILOCKS AND THE THREE BEARS

Retold and illustrated by
Bernadette Watts

North-South Books

In a cottage at the edge of a wood there once lived three bears:

A GREAT BIG BEAR

A MIDDLE-SIZED BEAR

and A TINY LITTLE BEAR.

On the other side of the wood lived a little girl and her parents. The little girl was called Goldilocks because of her golden hair.

One day the three bears went for a walk in the wood
while their breakfast porridge was cooling, and while they
were out, Goldilocks came to their cottage.

The door was open and she walked in. She looked around and saw that there was no one at home. On the table were three bowls of porridge:

A GREAT BIG BOWL

A MIDDLE-SIZED BOWL

and A TINY LITTLE BOWL.

Beside the table were three stools:
A GREAT BIG STOOL
A MIDDLE-SIZED STOOL
and A TINY LITTLE STOOL.

Goldilocks was hungry and the porridge smelled so good that she decided to taste it.

She picked up the great big spoon and took some porridge from the great big bowl, but it was much too hot and she burned her tongue.

Then she picked up the middle-sized spoon and tasted the porridge in the middle-sized bowl, but that was too cold.

So she tried the porridge in the tiny little bowl. That was just right – neither too hot nor too cold – and she had soon eaten it all.

Then, feeling tired, she looked around for a comfortable chair. First she tried the great big chair, but it was much too hard and she quickly jumped up again.

Then she tried the middle-sized chair, but that was too soft.

So she tried the tiny little chair and that was just right, neither too hard nor too soft, but when she leaned back the chair broke and she fell on the floor!

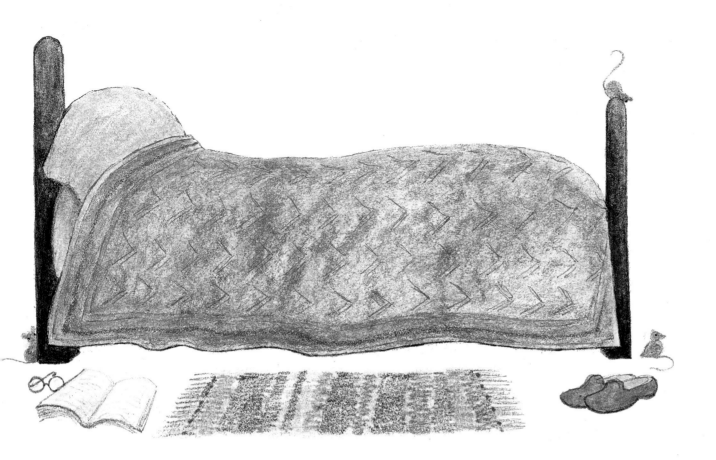

Now Goldilocks was very tired, so she went up the stairs into a bedroom. There she saw three beds:

A GREAT BIG BED

A MIDDLE-SIZED BED

and A TINY LITTLE BED.

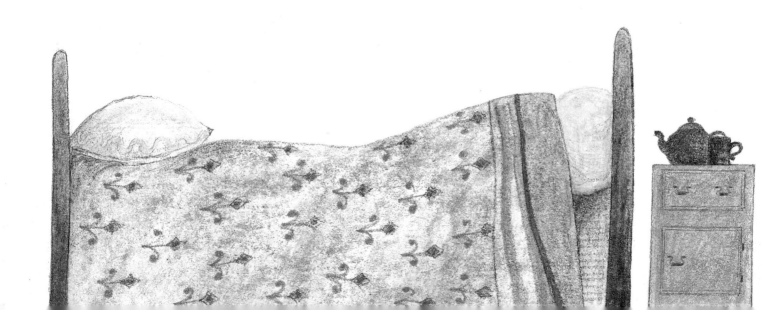

First she tried the great big bed, but it was much too high at the head.

Then she tried the middle-sized bed, but it was much too high at the foot.

So then she tried the tiny little bed. It was just right, and she fell fast asleep.

Soon the three bears came back from their walk.
They were hungry now and looking forward to eating
their porridge.

When the great big bear found his great big spoon in his
porridge bowl he roared, "Someone's been tasting my
porridge!"

Then the middle-sized bear found her middle-sized
spoon in her bowl, and she growled, "Someone's been
tasting my porridge!"

Then the tiny little bear found his tiny little spoon in his bowl
and the bowl was empty. "Someone's been tasting my
porridge," he squeaked, "and has eaten it all up!"

Then the great big bear looked at his chair. "Someone's been sitting on my chair!" he roared.

"And someone's been sitting on my chair!" growled the middle-sized bear.

"Someone's been sitting on my chair," squeaked the tiny little bear, "and has broken it!"

The three bears crept up to their bedroom. When the great big bear saw that his bedclothes were crumpled he roared, "Someone's been lying on my bed!" And the middle-sized bear growled, "Someone's been lying on my bed, too."

"Someone's been lying on my bed," squeaked the tiny little bear, "and here she is!"

Goldilocks woke up and was very frightened when she saw the three bears. She jumped out of the tiny little bed and ran out of the house.

She ran so fast that she soon reached the other side of the wood and was safe at home again with her parents. The bears tried to run after her but she was too quick for them and when they saw that they would never catch up with her they went grumbling and growling back to their cottage.

And Goldilocks never went to the bears' cottage again.

Copyright © 1984 Nord-Süd Verlag, Mönchaltorf, Switzerland
First published in Switzerland under the title
Goldilocks und die drei Bären
English text copyright © 1985 Rada Matija AG
Copyright English language edition under the imprint
North-South Books © 1985 Rada Matija AG, 8625 Gossau ZH, Switzerland

First published in Great Britain in 1984 under the imprint Abelard/North-
South by Abelard-Schuman Ltd and reissued in 1985 by North-South
Books, an imprint of Rada Matija AG. First published in the United States
in 1985 by North-South Books, an imprint of Rada Matija AG.

Reprinted for the United States, Great Britain, Canada, Australia and
New Zealand in 1986.

First English language paperback edition published in 1988.

Printed in Italy

Library of Congress Cataloging in Publication Data

Watts, Bernadette
  Goldilocks and the three bears.
  Translation of: Goldilocks und die drei Bären.
  Adaption of: Three bears.
  Summary: A little girl finds the empty home of the
three bears where she helps herself to food and goes to
sleep.
  [1. Folklore.   2. Bears—Fiction]   I. Three bears.
  II. Title.
  PZ8.1.W38Go   1985   398.2'1   [E]   85-7192

British Library Cataloguing in Publication Data

Goldilocks and the three bears
  I. Watts, Bernadette
  II. Goldilocks und die drei Bären. *English*
  833'.914[J]   P27

ISBN 3-85539-010-X